THIS WALKER BOOK BELONGS TO:

_____

_____

_____

_____

For Rosie Beth
M.W.

To Nan
L.H.

First published 1996 by Walker Books Ltd
87 Vauxhall Walk, London SE11 5HJ

This edition published 2001

2 4 6 8 10 9 7 5 3 1

Text © 1996 Martin Waddell
Illustrations © 1996 Leo Hartas

The right of Martin Waddell to be identified as author
of this work has been asserted by him in accordance with
the Copyright, Designs and Patents Act 1988

Printed in Hong Kong

British Library Cataloguing in Publication Data:
a catalogue record for this book
is available from the British Library

ISBN 0-7445-8279-2

Mimi
and the
Blackberry Pies

Written by
MARTIN WADDELL
Illustrated by
LEO HARTAS

WALKER BOOKS
AND SUBSIDIARIES

LONDON • BOSTON • SYDNEY

Mimi lived with her mouse sisters
and brothers beneath the big tree.
This is Mimi's house.

It was blackberry time in the hedge.
"I'm going to make blackberry pies,"
Mimi told her mouse sisters.

"We'll help you, Mimi!" her mouse sisters said. "We'll pick the best berries to go in the pies!" They all loved Mimi's blackberry pies.

Mimi's mouse sisters took their baskets
out to the hedge, and they started to pick
the juicy blackberries, but …

the berries were nice and they ate
a lot more than they picked.

They ate …

and they ate …   and they ate …

and they ate …

and they ate …   and they ate.

But they didn't pick many berries for Mimi.

"This isn't much help!" Mimi said, when she'd counted the berries they'd picked.

"We'll help you, Mimi," her mouse brothers cried. "We'll pick trillions of berries!" They all loved Mimi's blackberry pies.

Mimi's mouse brothers climbed up into
the hedge and got busy. But soon…
Some-brother-mouse splatted some-
other-brother-mouse with a berry!
Mouse-brother-splatting looked fun.
They forgot all about picking berries
for Mimi, and started mouse-splatting
each other instead.

They splatted …

and they splatted …

and they splatted …

and they splatted …

and they splatted.

But they didn't pick many berries for Mimi.

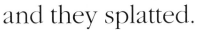

"This isn't much help!" Mimi sighed.
And she went out to the hedge and picked
all the berries she needed herself.

Mimi made blackberry pies.
A sweet berry smell drifted over
Mimi's sisters and brothers.

Their noses twitched …

and they twitched …

and they twitched …

and they twitched.

The rich berry smell was so good that …

Mimi's sisters and brothers ran to her house. Mimi came out with the pies that she'd made on a tray.

Mimi's blackberry pies were bursting with berries and juice.
"This time I'm sure that you'll help!" Mimi said. And her mouse sisters and brothers …

helped Mimi eat all her blackberry pies!

MARTIN WADDELL found his inspiration for **Mimi and the Blackberry Pies** in the countryside around his home. He says, "This story is all about my own family going blackberry picking. It is also about the wonderful scent of blackberries cooking, creeping through the kitchen the next day."

Martin Waddell is widely regarded as one of the finest contemporary writers of books for young people. Twice Winner of the Smarties Book Prize – for *Farmer Duck* and *Can't You Sleep, Little Bear?* – he also won the Kurt Maschler Award for *The Park in the Dark* and the Best Books for Babies Award for *Rosie's Babies*. Among his many other titles are *Owl Babies*; *Night Night, Cuddly Bear* and three other stories about Mimi. He was the Irish nominee for the 2000 Hans Christian Andersen Award. He lives with his wife Rosaleen in County Down, Northern Ireland.

LEO HARTAS says, "It was very fortunate that I did this book at the end of the summer because the bramble bushes were full of berries to paint from. But you have to be careful you don't splat yourself – the juice is a devil to wash out of your clothes!"

Leo Hartas has illustrated over twenty books, including the three other Mimi stories. He taught himself computer graphics and animation and now has a small company working on new ideas for interactive television and the Internet. Of his work he says, "All I have ever done has been because I enjoy it but I'm delighted to find children enjoy it too!" Leo lives in Brighton with his wife and three children.

Other Mimi stories by Martin Waddell and Leo Hartas

Mimi and the Dream House   0-7445-8274-1 (p/b) £3.99
Mimi and the Picnic   0-7445-8275-X (p/b) £3.99
Mimi's Christmas   0-7445-7213-4 (p/b) £4.99